Zelda and Ivy

and the

Boy Next Door

Zelda and Ivy
and the
Boy Next Door

L  KY

CANDLEWICK PRESS
CAMBRIDGE, MASSACHUSETTS

*To my father
Harvey Cooke McGee
1923 - 1998*

*Special thanks to my neighbor
Susan Carmel, and my nieces
Maia and Sofi Pothier,
for their inspiration*

Copyright © 1999 by Laura McGee Kvasnosky

First edition in this format 2008

The Library of Congress has cataloged the original hardcover edition as follows:

Kvasnosky, Laura McGee.
Zelda and Ivy and the boy next door / Laura McGee Kvasnosky. — 1st ed.
p. cm.
Summary: In three brief stories, two fox sisters meet the boy next door, play pirates, and camp out in the yard in sleeping bags.
ISBN 978-0-7636-0672-5 (original hardcover)
[1. Foxes—Fiction. 2. Sisters—Fiction.] I. Title.
PZ7.K975Zef 1999
[Fic]—dc21 98-23819

ISBN 978-0-7636-4004-0 (reformatted hardcover)

10 9 8 7 6 5 4 3 2 1

Printed in Singapore

This book was typeset in Galliard and hand-lettered by the author-illustrator. The illustrations were done in gouache resist.

Candlewick Press
2067 Massachusetts Avenue
Cambridge, Massachusetts 02140

visit us at www.candlewick.com

CONTENTS

Chapter One
ROMANCE

On Monday, Zelda and Ivy were playing dinosaur discovery when a new kid came over the fence.

"I'm Eugene," he said. "We're moving in next door."

"I'm Zelda," said Zelda, "the famous paleontologist." She dumped sand on her sister. "Ivy's a stegosaurus," she added. "I'm going to dig her up."

"Do you want to come over and see my Band-Aid collection?" asked Eugene.

"I guess so," said Zelda.

Eugene kept his Band-Aids in a binder.

"Most of them haven't even been used," he said. "The Superfox Band-Aid is my favorite."

He smiled at Zelda. "But you can have it."

"Thanks," said Zelda.

Eugene sighed. "Will you marry me?"

Zelda rolled her eyes. Ivy raised her eyebrows. "I'll think about it," said Zelda.

On Tuesday, Eugene came over very early.

"Have you decided?" he asked.

"Not yet," said Zelda. "We have to clean our room."

"Can I help?" asked Eugene.

Ivy put away toys.

Eugene picked up books.

Zelda relaxed on the top bunk.

"Clean under the bed," she reminded them. Eugene found an old doll under the bed.

"Clarissa!" exclaimed Zelda. She grabbed the doll.

"Now will you marry me?" asked

Eugene.

"I'll think about it," said Zelda.

On Wednesday, Zelda and Ivy were
playing castle when Eugene came over
the fence.

"Now?" he pleaded.

"Can you battle a dragon?" asked Zelda.

"No," said Eugene sadly.

On Thursday, Zelda and Ivy played cowgirls. Zelda let Eugene be the cow.

"Will you marry me now?" he mooed.

"I'm still thinking about it," said Zelda.

On Friday, Zelda was mixing pink
lemonade when Eugene came over.

"Don't dare mention it," she told him.

"We're going to have a lemonade stand,"
explained Ivy. "Want to help?"

Eugene set up the chairs and table. Ivy
painted the sign.

When the lemonade
stand was ready,
Zelda sat on the
cool porch with
her library book.

Eugene and Ivy sat in the hot sun and
sold lemonade. They made four dollars
and fifty cents.

Eugene handed over the money to
Zelda. He looked at her hopefully.
"Now will you marry me?" he asked.

Zelda jiggled the coins in her pocket. She handed a dollar each to Eugene and Ivy.

"No," she said and went into the house.

Eugene slumped down on the porch steps.

Ivy sat next to him. She patted his knee. "It'll be okay," she said.

Eugene sniffed a few times, then looked at Ivy. He pulled a Superfox Band-Aid out of his pocket and offered it to her.

"Will *you* marry me?" he asked.

Chapter Two
PiRaTeS

"Thwack," yelled Zelda as she slashed acorns with her pirate sword. "Thwack, thwack!"

"Why can't I play pirate?" asked Ivy.

"Because methinks you don't know how to talk like a pirate," called Zelda from the crow's nest. She shinnied down to the tree fort ship.

"Yo, ho, ho!" Zelda shouted to Eugene.

They punched their paws together.

"Yo, ho, ho!" he shouted in return.

Ivy stood under the tree.

"Oooh-arrgh!" she said. "See? I can talk like a pirate."

"Sorry, matey," said Eugene. "Captain's orders."

Ivy scuffed across the lawn.

"I can too play pirate," she said to herself.

She went in the house and got her bottle cap collection. Back outside, she put a few bottle caps in her pocket, then buried the tin in the garden.

"Gold doubloons," she said loudly.

Eugene and Zelda didn't notice. They were arguing. Ivy perked up her ears. She heard Zelda order Eugene to walk the plank.

"No," wailed Eugene.

Ivy hopped up on the picnic bench.

"Shiver me timbers," she shouted. "I will walk the plank."

Zelda and Eugene looked down at her.

"But if I walk the plank," Ivy said, "methinks you'll never know where the secret treasure is buried."

Zelda and Eugene scrambled down the tree.

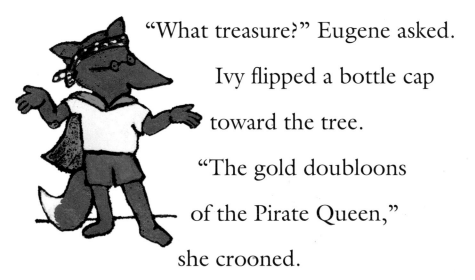

"What treasure?" Eugene asked.

Ivy flipped a bottle cap toward the tree.

"The gold doubloons of the Pirate Queen," she crooned.

"Well," said Zelda, twitching her whiskers, "maybe we could use a second mate."

Ivy smiled.

"Second mate," ordered Zelda, "dig up that treasure."

"Aye, aye, Captain," crowed Ivy.

But Eugene was not so happy. "Then who will walk the plank?" he asked.

"I'll decide that later," said Zelda.

"I think I'll go home now," said Eugene.

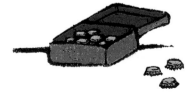

Chapter Three
Camping Out

Ivy gave Zelda's sleeping bag a tug.

"Zelda," she said, "are you awake?"

"Rats," mumbled Zelda. "I am now."

"I can't sleep," said Ivy. "I wish we'd invited Eugene."

"No way," said Zelda. "Sisters only."

"Could you at least sing a song to help me sleep?" asked Ivy.

"Okay," said Zelda, "if you promise to shut your eyes."

Ivy promised. Zelda sang "The Star-Spangled Banner."

Ivy's eyes popped open.

"I still can't sleep," she said. "Could you hold my paw and sing one more?"

"Okay," said Zelda. "But remember— keep those eyes shut."

Ivy shut her eyes. Zelda held Ivy's paw and sang "Take Me Out to the Ball Game." She finished softly and patted Ivy's paw.

Ivy's eyes popped open again.

"I still can't sleep," she said. "Could you sing just one more?"

"I'm tired of singing," said Zelda. "Let's look for shooting stars. Whoever sees one first gets to make a wish."

The fox sisters snuggled down in their sleeping bags and looked up into the sparkling night.

"There's one," said Ivy. "I saw it first."

"Rats," said Zelda.

"Here's my wish," said Ivy. "I wish you would sing me another song."

"Oh, all right," said Zelda. She sang "The Ants Go Marching One by One."

Ivy was quiet at the end of the song.

Zelda quickly looked for another

shooting star. She saw the thin curve of a

new moon rising and the sugared stars of

the Milky Way. Finally, another star zipped

across the sky.

"That one's mine," said Zelda, "so I get

to make the wish. I wish you would sing

ME a song."

Ivy didn't say a word.

"Ivy?" asked Zelda.

She shined her flashlight on Ivy's face.

"Ivy?" she said louder.

Ivy rolled over and mumbled in her
sleep.

"Rats," said Zelda.